Dr. Crisp Media Center
50 Arlington Street
Nashua, NH 03060

OBSOLETE/
SURPLUS
Nashua School District # 42

Published by Doubleday, a division of
Bantam Doubleday Dell Publishing Group, Inc.
666 Fifth Avenue, New York, New York 10103
Published by arrangement with William Collins Sons & Co. Ltd

Doubleday and the portrayal of an anchor with a dolphin
are trademarks of Doubleday, a division of
Bantam Doubleday Dell Publishing Group, Inc.

Library of Congress Cataloging-in-Publication Data
Hawkins, Colin.
Crocodile creek: the cry in the night / by Colin and Jacqui
Hawkins.—1st ed.
p.   cm.
Summary: Relates the troubles of the Crocker family when Baby
Crocker starts teething and chews everything in sight.
ISBN 0-385-24979-9; ISBN 0-385-24980-2 (lib. bdg.)
[1. Crocodiles—Fiction.   2. Humorous stories.]   I. Hawkins,
Jacqui.   II. Title.
PZ7.H313513Cr   1989
[E]—dc19   88-28269
CIP
AC

Text copyright © 1988 by Colin and Jacqui Hawkins
Illustrations copyright © 1988 by Colin Hawkins

PRINTED IN HONG KONG
ALL RIGHTS RESERVED
FIRST EDITION IN THE UNITED STATES OF AMERICA, 1989

Crocodile Creek

The Cry in the Night

by Colin and Jacqui Hawkins

⚓

DOUBLEDAY
NEW YORK   LONDON   TORONTO   SYDNEY   AUCKLAND

On their houseboat in Crocodile Creek, the Crocker family was fast asleep. Zzzzz!

All except Baby Croc, who had woken up. He began to roar, "Aaaaaw! Aaaaaw!"

Baby Crocker was not well and his crying woke up Mum, Dad, his big sister, his older brother and Gran. In fact, he woke up everyone.

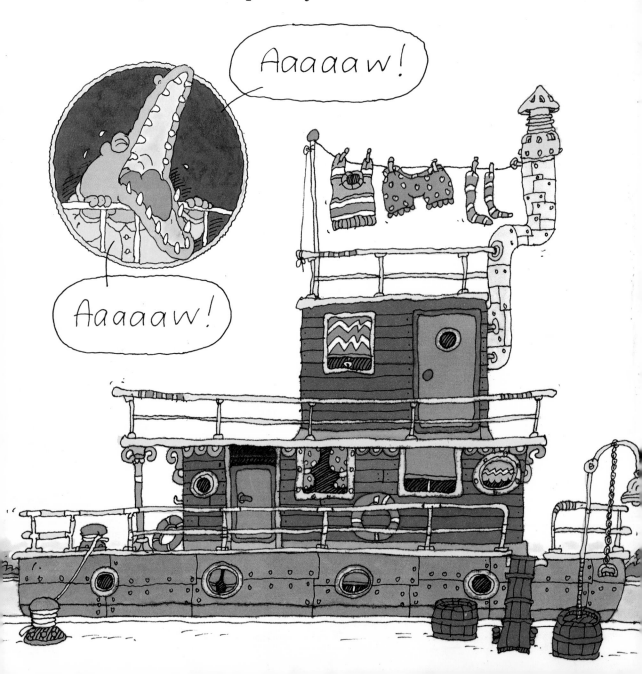

By breakfast time, Baby Crocker had stopped crying but he was not happy. He was feeling snappy and wanted to bite everything in sight. He bit the cereal box and he bit his sister's comic. He chewed his brother's math book, Mum's hat, Dad's gloves and Gran's flippers.

"I'm taking this baby to the doctor," said Dad. Mum took the other children to school and Gran went windsurfing.

At the Baby Clinic, the noise was terrible. There were baby crocodiles playing everywhere.

Some were fighting and others were biting. Some were spotty and some felt grotty. One was even on the potty!

At last Dad and Baby Crocker saw Doctor Croc. She looked into Baby Crocker's ears and into his eyes.

Then she looked into his mouth. She took his temperature and listened to his chest.

"There's nothing wrong with Baby," she said.

"But he has a big tooth coming through, which may be making him cross."

Baby Crocker waved good-bye and they set off for home.

Back on the houseboat Dad made himself a cup of tea and gave the baby his lunch. It was Baby Crocker's favourite – fish fingers and chips with lots of tomato ketchup!

Dad settled down to read *The Creek Courier*.
"You've been chewing this again, haven't you?"
he said. "Look at all these holes."

CLANG! CLANG!
The houseboat bell rang.

Dr. Crisp Media Center
50 Arlington Street
Nashua, NH 03060

It was Postman Croc with a huge parcel. Dad Crocker was pleased. In the parcel was a new propeller for the houseboat engine.

Meanwhile Baby Crocker had finished his lunch
and bitten the leg off the table.

After that he toddled out onto the deck.
    . . . He nibbled at a door, chewed a life preserver and
then he found a rope. It was the mooring rope – the
rope that tied the houseboat to the riverbank.
With three bites Baby Crocker snapped right through it!

The houseboat began to drift away from the riverbank. Baby Crocker giggled and waved.

"Oh no!" cried Dad.

He and the postman stared in horror as the boat and baby floated out into the fast-flowing river.

Dad leaped into his row boat, grabbed the oars and rowed as fast as he could. Dad Crocker rowed and rowed.

"This is an emergency!" he shouted.

But Dad had forgotten something. The row boat was still tied up! TWANG! THUMP! Dad was thrown tail over teeth into the bottom of the boat.

Dad clambered to his claws. Now the houseboat was even farther downstream!

"Oh no, it's heading for Fatal Falls!" cried Dad.

If only he could throw the rope and hook onto the houseboat. But he was too far away!

Dad was helpless and Baby Crocker was now in great danger.

SWISH! Suddenly Gran came by on her windsurfer.

"Give me that!" she cried. Snatching the rope and hook, she skimmed across the river after the houseboat.

WHOOSH! Gran sped nearer and nearer to the houseboat, but the houseboat was getting closer and closer to the falls.

Would she make it in time?

"Hold on!" she called to Baby Crocker. And she whirled the rope and hook round and round her head.

The houseboat was now on the very edge . . . Gran hurled the rope with all her might.

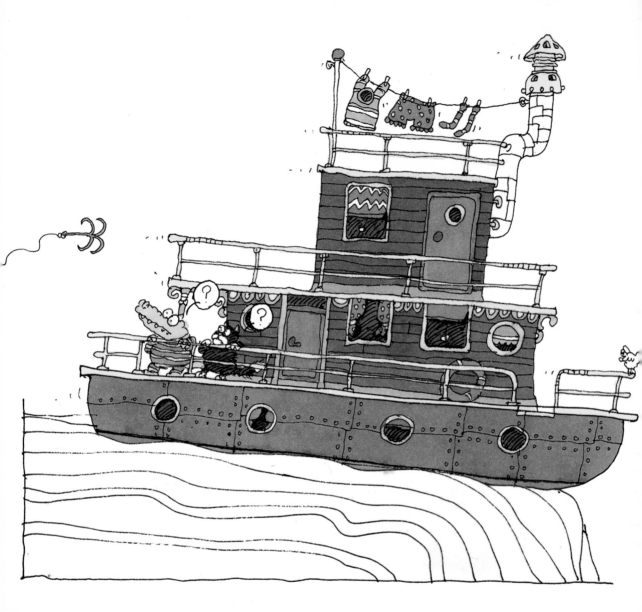

The rope whizzed through the air.
The front of the houseboat tipped over
the edge of the dreaded Fatal Falls.

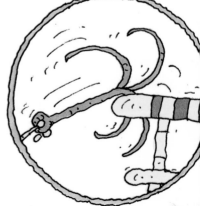

CLUNK! Just in time, the hook caught onto the rail.

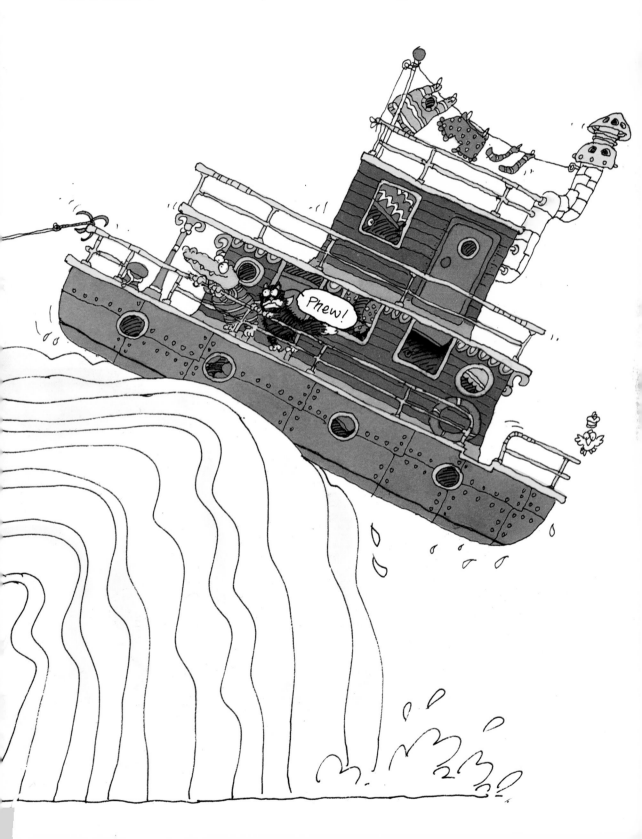

TWANG! The rope went very tight and the houseboat stopped.

TWANG! The rope on Dad's row boat went tight too.

BI-ONG! Dad shot up into the air.

Baby Crocker laughed and waved! Dad Crocker was very funny sometimes.

Back on the riverbank Postman Croc, Mum Crocker
and everyone heaved and heaved on the rope.
First they pulled in Dad and his row boat.

Then they all hauled the houseboat and Baby
Crocker safely back to the riverbank.
"My baby!" called Mum, and she sighed with relief.

Dad tied up the houseboat to the riverbank.
"I'll use a chain this time!" he said.
Then Gran came sailing in.
"Hurray!" cheered everyone. "Well done, Gran!"

Mum Crocker gave Baby Crocker a big hug and
a big kiss.
   Baby Crocker smiled a big smile and there, shining out,
was a brand-new tooth!